My
Adorable

Kitten

For Dad, the reason why all dads in my books are funny

Scholastic Children's Books
An imprint of Scholastic Ltd
Euston House, 24 Eversholt Street, London, NW1 1DB, UK
Registered office: Westfield Road, Southam, Warwickshire, CV47 0RA
SCHOLASTIC and associated logos are trademarks and/or
registered trademarks of Scholastic Inc.

First published in the UK by Scholastic Ltd, 2016

Text copyright © Scholastic Ltd, 2016

ISBN 978 1407 16247 8

A CIP catalogue record for this book
is available from the British Library.

Printed by CPI Group (UK) Ltd, Croydon, CR0 4YY
Papers used by Scholastic Children's Books are made
from wood grown in sustainable forests.

1 3 5 7 9 10 8 6 4 2

www.scholastic.co.uk

My
Adorable
Kitten

Sarah Hawkins

■SCHOLASTIC

1

"Guess what!" Nia shouted as she and her best friend Charlotte ran out of school. They rushed over to where Granny was waiting with baby Kayla in her buggy.

"What?" Granny asked.

"We know what the end of term show is going to be!" Nia said breathlessly. "It's *The Wizard of Oz!*"

"I can't wait!" Charlotte said with a squeal. "I want to be the Wicked Witch of the West!"

Nia grinned. The witch was a fun part with lots of stomping around and cackling. She was sure Charlotte would get it.

1

Charlotte screwed her face up into an ugly grimace and gave a screechy laugh. "Mwa ha ha ha, I'll get you, my pretty!" she said in her witchiest voice.

Kayla jumped and her bottom lip wobbled.

"Oh, no!" Charlotte said.

"It's OK, it's only Charlotte," Nia told her. Both girls crouched down to comfort Kayla. Nia kissed her sister on her chubby cheek. Kayla was only two and she was so cute. She had dark skin and dark brown eyes just like Nia, but her curly hair was tied up in two little bunches, rather than the neat braids Nia had. She wriggled in her buggy and pushed herself forward, pointing at a dog. "Tat! Tat!" she said.

"What's she saying, Granny?" Nia asked.

Granny rolled her eyes. "Her childminder's cat has had kittens, and now she thinks everything is a cat. Even her new book is all about a cat," Granny said, showing Nia a picture book. On the front was an adorable grey fluffy cat wearing a tiara.

"Pearl the Princess Cat!" Nia read out. Kayla wriggled in her buggy happily.

"Tat," she agreed, pointing across the playground again.

"But that's a dog, Kayla," Nia said, pointing at the animal. "D-o-g."

"Tat!" Kayla said delightedly.

Nia and Charlotte laughed.

"Come on, let's go home," Granny said. Charlotte often came back to their house after school because her mum didn't finish work until later.

"So, what is the Wizard of Woz?" Granny said as they started walking.

"Wizard of Oz, silly!" Nia laughed. Granny was from Sierra Leone, and even though she'd lived in the UK since Nia's mum was born, she said funny things sometimes.

"*The Wizard of Oz* is about a girl called Dorothy," Nia explained. "She gets taken to a magical world called Oz by a cyclone, and has to go on a journey to find the Wizard to ask him to send her back home."

"A wicked witch tries to stop her," Charlotte said, making her witch face again. This time Kayla giggled.

"But with help from her friends – a cowardly lion, a tin man and a scarecrow – Dorothy goes home," Nia finished.

"Oh, and she has a little dog called Toto," Charlotte added, flipping her long brown hair over her shoulder.

"There are lots of costumes. And songs too," Nia said happily. She loved acting. She and Charlotte had always played pretend games with each other, ever since they met at playgroup when they were almost as tiny as Kayla. Drama was just like playing pretend, except people clapped when you finished. Nia knew lots of other people were shy and hated performing, but she thought it was so much fun!

"What part do you want, Nia?" Granny looked at Nia, her brown eyes twinkling.

"Dorothy!" Charlotte said, staring at Nia. "You want to be Dorothy, don't you?"

Nia nodded. "Yes! But it's the main part – I don't know if I'll get it."

Granny stopped pushing the buggy and put her arm around Nia. "You can do *anything* if you try hard enough," she said. "Now, come on, I've made Benny cake for you."

"Yum!" Charlotte grinned.

Nia smiled too. She remembered the first time Charlotte had had Benny cake and been confused, because it was more like a sesame-seed biscuit than a cake. But it was delicious! Now her best friend loved Granny's snacks.

"We'll have a snack, and then you can

practise for me and Kayla. We'd like that, wouldn't we, Kayla?"

Kayla leaned forward in her buggy. "Tat!" she said excitedly.

Something ran across the path in front of them. It *was* a cat this time!

"Good girl, Kayla," Nia laughed.

"Black cats are lucky," Granny said.

Nia crossed her fingers as the cat ran into a garden and started washing its paws. If she was going to get the main part, she'd need all the luck she could get!

"Come quickly!" Jade shrieked across the school playground.

Charlotte and Nia were sitting on the grass eating their packed lunches. Charlotte rolled her eyes. Jade Miller was in their drama class, and she was a massive show-off. The girls watched as Jade rushed across to her friends, her shoulder-length blonde hair flying out behind her.

"The cast list for *The Wizard of Oz* is up!" Jade yelled, pushing her purple glasses back on her nose. "I bet I know what part I got!" She and her friends sped across the playground, squealing with excitement.

Nia swallowed her mouthful of lunch awkwardly. Suddenly she felt sick with nerves. Charlotte looked at her, her eyes wide, and Nia knew she was feeling the same way. "I bet you've got it," she said reassuringly. "Your audition was brilliant."

"Yours too," Charlotte said.

"What are you waiting for?" their friend Emma said. "Go and find out!"

Nia got to her feet nervously.

"Fingers crossed!" Emma said.

Charlotte grabbed Nia's hand as they ran over to the school hall. "I'm so nervous!" she whispered.

"Me too!" Nia said.

There was a big crowd around the noticeboard. Jade was standing in the middle, shrieking and squealing excitedly.

"I can't look!" Charlotte said.

"I'll do it," Nia told her. She marched up to the sign. *Please, please,* she thought, crossing her fingers as hard as she could.

Dorothy – she read – Jade Miller.

"I can't believe I got it!" Jade shrieked nearby.

Nia felt her eyes fill up with tears. She looked down the list. Wicked Witch – Charlotte Banks. She wiped her eyes and put a smile on her face.

Charlotte was standing anxiously. Nia turned to her. "You're the wicked witch!" she said with a smile.

"I am?" Charlotte squealed, jumping up and down.

Nia nodded.

"What about you?" Charlotte asked.

Nia could only shake her head. "I didn't get Dorothy."

"Oh no!" Charlotte stopped bouncing. "But you must have got something!"

"I didn't look," Nia said.

Charlotte pushed her way back to the notice. Nia trailed after her.

"There!" Charlotte pointed. Cowardly Lion – Nia Madaki.

Nia bit her lip to stop herself from crying. Across the playground, Jade was twirling happily and talking loudly about how good she was going to be. Nia felt the tears prickle in her eyes and wiped her sleeve over them hurriedly.

"That's a really big part," Charlotte said.

Nia nodded, but inside she was shouting, *I don't want to be the Lion. I want to be Dorothy!*

2

Nia was still upset when her Mum picked her up from school. When they got home her family were all sitting around the kitchen table. Granny was cooking and Dad was feeding Kayla in her high chair. The house smelt like Granny's delicious stew, but Nia wasn't hungry at all; her tummy was too sad.

"Well?" Dad said. Mum shook her head. Nia looked at her family's faces and burst into tears.

"Come here," Dad said, opening up his arms. Nia went over and he gave her a hug. He was still wearing his work overalls and the material was scratchy but familiar. He smelt like car oil and Dad, and Nia buried her face in his shoulder.

"Tell them about the lion," Mum prompted.

"I have to be the Cowardly Lion!" Nia said with a sniffle.

"But that's great!" Dad said, rubbing her back. "That's a brilliant part!"

"No, it's not," Nia said. "Jade is Dorothy."

Granny came over and held out the wooden spoon for Nia to lick. "Jade will be Dorothy, and you will be the best lion ever," she said firmly. "In Sierra Leone we are very proud of lions. Do you know what Sierra Leone means? It means Lion Mountains."

Nia smiled, but she still felt sad. "I really wanted to be Dorothy," she said.

"Granny's right," Dad said, looking at her seriously, his brown eyes kind. "You want to be an actress when you grow up, don't you?"

Nia nodded, then felt the tears come again. "But how can I be an actress if I'm not good enough to be Dorothy?"

"You can't be the lead every time," Dad said. "When you're an actress you're not always going to get the part you want, but you just have to play the part you have the very best you can. You be the best lion you can be."

"Muma, down!" Kayla called from her high chair.

Mum wiped Kayla's face and picked her up out of her high chair, then came over to plant a kiss on Nia's head.

"Besides, you know who's going to love your costume?" she said, with an enormous grin. "Kayla! Her big sister is going to be an enormous cat!"

"Tat?" Kayla said curiously.

Nia burst into laughter. "Yes, Kayla. I'm going to be a cat!"

"Nia!"

Nia ran downstairs to find out what Mum wanted. "I need to go and get something from Kayla's childminder," she said, with a funny look on her face.

"Can I stay here with Dad and Granny?" Nia asked.

"No, I need your help," Mum said, mysteriously.

"What for?" Nia asked, but Mum didn't answer. Things got even stranger when Mum put Kayla in her car seat. They normally walked to her childminder's house. It was a nice walk through the park and Nia loved pointing out all the dogs and squirrels to Kayla as they passed.

"Oh!" Nia suddenly remembered something. "The childminder has kittens, doesn't she? Can I see them?"

"Oh, I don't know," Mum said, her brown eyes sparkling. "We'll have to ask. Come on!"

Nia shook her head; her mum was acting really strangely. She got into the front seat. "What's going on?" she asked Kayla. But Kayla just grabbed her own foot and put it in her mouth.

Mum seemed excited all the way to the childminder's house. When Mrs Wilson opened the door, she looked excited too. *What is going on?* Nia thought.

"Hello, Nia," Mrs Wilson said, "and hello, sweetie." She took Kayla from Mum and gave her a big hug.

Kayla patted her face and Mrs Wilson laughed. Kayla started wriggling in her arms and pointing towards the lounge door. "Tat, tat!"

"Yes, that's right," Mrs Wilson told her. She put Kayla down and she toddled towards the door.

"Go on," Mum said.

Nia followed Kayla into the lounge. There, in a big playpen, was a stripy white-and-grey cat and four gorgeous kittens!

"Awwww!" Nia breathed.

The mother cat lay back sleepily and just blinked at them, but the four babies scampered around in the playpen. They were much fluffier than their mum, and they all had different markings. There were two stripy ones, a completely white one, and the fluffiest one of all was grey with a white tummy.

As Nia went in, they scrambled over to the edge of the playpen, looking up at her with their bright green eyes.

Kayla toddled up to the playpen and stretched her hand over, trying to touch them.

The white one came up and sniffed her fingers curiously. "Tat!" Kayla shouted in delight, and the kitten dashed away.

"They're so cute! What are they called?" Nia asked Mrs Wilson. She couldn't take her eyes off them!

"That one's Posy," Mrs Wilson said, pointing at the white one, who was playing with a toy mouse. "I'm keeping her. But the other three will be named by their new families."

"They were born ten weeks ago, so they're old enough now to go to homes of their own," Mum explained.

They were the most adorable things Nia had ever seen. "Aw! I wish we could have one," she said, half to herself.

"Why do you think we're here?" Mum said.

Nia turned to look at her in amazement. Mum and Mrs Wilson were grinning from ear to ear.

"What?" Nia gasped.

"We've come to take home our cat!" Mum said.

"What?" Nia shrieked again. She looked at the kittens in amazement. "Which one?"

"Any one you and Kayla want, apart from Posy," Mrs Wilson said.

Nia looked at the kittens. She couldn't believe one of them was going to be hers.

They are all so cute! she thought. *How am I ever going to decide?*

Mrs Wilson handed Nia a cat toy: a fish on a long piece of string. Nia dangled it over the playpen, and giggled as she realized she was fishing for cats. The two stripy ones were curled up with their mum, and the white fluffy one was licking its paws, but the grey fluffy one sat up as soon as it saw the fish toy dangling around. It trotted over then stopped a little way away from the toy, watching as Nia wriggled it.

Nia waggled the fish again. The kittens were all gorgeous, but she couldn't stop watching the fluffy grey one. It rushed over to the toy and sat on its fluffy bum, putting one paw in the air to try and catch the fish. It was the most adorable thing Nia had ever seen!

"You girls can get into the pen if you want," Mrs Wilson said.

Nia carefully climbed over and sat cross-legged.

Mum put Kayla over the side and on to the mat. She tried to race over to the kittens, but Mum caught her. "Sit nicely," Mum said.

Kayla plonked herself down on her bum. Mrs Wilson scooped up the grey kitten and put it on Nia's lap.

Nia could hardly breathe as she held on to the warm, wriggly little kitten. It was so tiny and so cute! She stroked the kitten's soft head and it cuddled up to her happily, nudging its head into her hand.

"Me, me," Kayla strained to stroke it.

"Gently," Mum told her.

Kayla softly patted the kitten.

Mrs Wilson handed Nia one of the stripy ones, then picked up the other stripy one and put that on Nia as well. She was covered in kittens! She felt like she didn't have enough hands to stroke them all.

One of the stripy kittens climbed all over her legs and the other one jumped straight off and ran back over to its mum, but the little grey one turned around in a circle and snuggled down on Nia's lap, with its tiny tail tucked neatly around its paws.

Nia daren't move in case she disturbed the tiny kitten. She put out her hand and gently stroked its soft fur. It felt warm and the fur was delicate and so soft. The baby cat had a grey back, bright green eyes and small ears. As Nia watched, it yawned, and Nia could see its pink tongue and pointy white teeth.

Mum shuffled closer with Kayla, and

Kayla gently stroked the kitten's back. The kitten wriggled happily, then flipped over to show them its fluffy white tummy.

"That one is a little girl," said Mrs Wilson.

As they stroked her, the kitten started to purr – surprisingly loudly for such a little cat. Nia could feel the rumbles going all the way through her body.

"Tat mine," Kayla muttered determinedly.

"You want this one?" Nia asked, looking at her baby sister.

"Tat!" Kayla said. Nia looked at all the other kittens, and then down at the one in her lap. She gently ran her fingers through the kitten's soft fur, and it purred even louder in delight. Nia giggled. Kayla was right – this one was theirs!

"Have you decided?" Mrs Wilson asked.

Nia nodded. "This is our cat." She felt a flood of joy. "This is OUR cat! We have a cat!" she said happily.

Mum grinned at her. "Granny and Dad are setting up her bed and litter tray and everything for her at home, and I've got a cat basket in the boot of the car."

"I can't believe we're going home with a cat!" Nia said.

Mum kissed the top of her head. "Well, Kayla was in love with them, and I know you've always wanted one. When Mrs Wilson said she needed to find homes for them, it seemed perfect."

"What are you going to name her?" said Mrs Wilson.

Kayla opened her mouth, but Nia interrupted. "We're not calling her Tat!" she said.

On the way home Nia held the cat carrier tightly on her lap to keep the kitten nice and safe. Kayla was wriggling in her car seat, so Nia turned the basket to let her baby sister see in though the wire. Inside the kitten was looking around curiously. She hadn't meowed at all yet.

Nia poked her fingers through the mesh and stroked her new cat's soft head, as the kitten snuggled up to her hand.

"I don't know what we should call her," Nia said.

"We'll think of something that suits her

once we know what her personality is like," Mum said.

Nia looked at the kitten and felt like crying. She couldn't believe she was really hers. She looked up and met Mum's eyes in the car mirror.

"Thank you, Mum," she said. "I love her already."

Mum smiled. "You're welcome, Nia. Just make sure you help look after her."

"I will," Nia promised with all her heart.

As soon as they pulled into the driveway, Dad flung the front door open.

Everyone got out of the car. Mum took the cat carrier, and Nia held Kayla's hand so she could toddle up the pathway.

"Thank you SO MUCH!" Nia flung her arms around Dad's middle when they got to him.

"You like your surprise, then?" he said with a grin.

"I LOVE her!" Nia told him.

Dad picked Kayla up and gave her a cuddle. "And you like your cat too?"

Kayla wriggled and giggled in his arms and Dad pulled up her T-shirt and blew a raspberry on her tummy. She squealed with delight as he carried her into the house.

Mum followed behind with the cat carrier.

"We've set everything up in the lounge," Dad told her.

Nia went into the lounge excitedly. This morning it had looked the same as usual, with two sofas, two tall bookcases, and the TV in one corner. But now there was a comfy blue basket, a scratching post and a litter tray too!

"We won't keep everything in here for ever," Mum explained. "But kittens need to stay in a small space to start with so they don't get scared."

Nia thought about the playpen at Mrs Wilson's and nodded. Everything must seem huge to such a tiny cat!

"Mama, the cat's here," Mum called up the stairs.

Granny came down, clapping her hands with excitement. "Oooh! Let me see!" she said enthusiastically.

Once everyone was in the lounge with the door shut, Mum put the cat carrier on the floor and opened the wire door. For a second nothing happened.

"I've got an idea," Nia said. Mrs Wilson had given them the dangling fish toy because it was their kitten's favourite. Nia grabbed it, then crouched down on her knees, and dangled it outside the cat carrier. A tiny paw came out and batted it! Nia pulled the fish toy further away. Suddenly the little kitten galloped out! She pawed at the fish and Nia let her have it. Then the little cat looked around in amazement, as if she'd just realized she wasn't in the carrier any more.

"Oh! She's lovely!" Granny said.

"Great choice, girls," Dad agreed.

"Tat!" Kayla wriggled to be let down, but when Dad did so she wobbled after the kitten so fast that the tiny cat jumped back into the cat carrier nervously.

"Here, gently, gently," Dad said, showing Kayla how to pet the kitten. "We're relying on you to help look after her," he told Nia. "Kayla's too little, but you're old enough to help."

"I know," Nia said. "I will, I promise." She sat down next to the cat carrier. From inside, two green eyes peeked out. Nia put her hand in and gently touched the little cat. She'd always thought that cats liked being stroked down their backs, but the kitten seemed to especially like being tickled around her ears. When Nia rubbed her head, she nuzzled up into Nia's hand as if she was asking for more.

Everyone watched as the fluffy kitten stepped out of the carrier again and started sniffing around all of her new things. She took a drink out of her water bowl, her tiny pink tongue lapping at the water, and Nia felt a rush of happiness. "Aww!" she squealed. "She's just perfect!"

"What will we call her?" Granny said.

"How about Mouser," Dad suggested.

Nia screwed up her face. "That's a terrible name!"

"I say Leo," Granny said. "That means lion, like in your play."

"But that's a boy's name!" Nia protested.

"Nia's picking the name," Mum said, "but she doesn't have to do it right this second."

Nia thought hard. She was sure she'd

seen a picture of a grey fluffy kitten somewhere recently... Suddenly she remembered. She jumped up and went to Kayla's buggy, rummaging around until she found her sister's new book. "Look!" she said delightedly. "They look so similar. Well, apart from the tiara!"

"Pearl the princess cat!" Mum exclaimed.

"Maybe that's what we should call her," Granny said. "Pearl!"

Everyone looked at the kitten. She stepped delicately into the litter tray – and then started scratching in it, sending bits of kitty litter flying everywhere.

Spotting them watching her, she turned and gazed innocently at the family.

Everyone laughed. Pearl might be named after a princess, but she was more of a troublemaker than she looked!

The next morning, Nia woke up to a funny scrabbly sound. She opened her eyes and blinked sleepily. Something was clicking over the boards of her bedroom floor. Then something tugged at her covers.

"Five minutes more, Mum," Nia said, sleepily. Then there was a thump and something landed on top of her. Nia lifted her head to take a look. Pearl was sitting on her tummy!

Pearl looked up, her big eyes wide. "What are you doing up here?" Nia gasped. "You're meant to stay in the lounge!"

Pearl walked up Nia's body and nudged Nia's face with the side of her head, like she was asking for a stroke.

"Oh, Pearl!" Nia stroked her and she cuddled up, purring happily. She made a loud noise for such a little cat. Nia couldn't tell her off, she was just too sweet!

"Mum will be wondering where you are!"

she said. She tickled Pearl under her chin, and the little cat flopped over on to her back, putting her legs in the air.

Nia heard footsteps outside her room. "Mum!" she called.

Granny stuck her head round the door. "What is little Pearl doing up here?" she exclaimed. "Did you get her?" She tutted.

"No!" Nia said. "I just woke up. She came to find me!"

"I can't believe she climbed all those stairs!" Granny sat down on the end of the bed and Pearl raced over to see her. "She must love you very much already!"

Nia smiled in delight. But the next thing Granny said made her pout.

"Time to get ready for school," Granny said.

"No!" Nia said, snuggling back under the duvet. As she moved her toes under the covers, they caught Pearl's attention. Pearl jumped to the end of the bed and pounced on the wriggling duvet. Nia giggled in delight as the kitten scrabbled on the covers.

Granny patted Nia's leg. "Now, school. Come on, get *up*!"

"Why did we have to get her on a Sunday?" Nia moaned. "Now I won't be able to see her properly until next weekend!"

"She'll be here when you get back from school," Granny said, picking up Pearl and cradling her in her arms. "That is the good thing about her living here now. Hurry up and come downstairs, I'll make breakfast."

Granny hurried downstairs with Pearl in her arms.

Nia jumped out of bed and started pulling her uniform on. Last night had been one of the best evenings ever. She had spent the evening playing with Pearl until the little cat had fallen asleep on her lap. Her family had watched the TV, but Nia couldn't tear her eyes away from the softly sleeping kitten. She had gorgeous little pink pads on the underside of her paws, and she made adorable snuffly snoring sounds as she slept.

When it was Nia's bedtime, Dad had scooped Pearl up and put her in her basket, and she'd barely stirred.

"It's been a big day for her," Mum had said.

Nia had smiled. It had been a big day for her too. Now she had a cat that she would love for ever!

Nia shook her head as she realized she was daydreaming when she could be playing with Pearl. She finished dressing as fast as she could, then ran downstairs. She couldn't believe Pearl had climbed all this way!

She opened the lounge door carefully. Pearl was inside, sitting in her basket, but she jumped up and trotted over to Nia when she came in.

Nia shut the lounge door carefully behind her and bent down to give Pearl a stroke. Pearl was wriggling happily when Granny and Mum came in with Kayla.

"I thought we could eat breakfast in here today," Mum grinned, passing Nia a bowl. "Although we can probably let Pearl out around the whole house soon; she's obviously not scared if she's already started exploring on her own."

Nia sat on the sofa to eat her cereal. Pearl was watching interestedly. She looked at the sofa, then crouched and wiggled her little bum. "She's going to jump!" Granny said with a chuckle.

Pearl gave a big leap and jumped on to the sofa next to Nia. She shook herself proudly, then climbed over to Nia's lap, trying to put her nose in her bowl. She really was a mischievous little kitten.

"Don't let her eat any," Mum warned.

"Aw, but cats like milk, though, and it's so cute!" Nia said.

"Well, firstly, it's not hygienic to share your breakfast," Mum said. "Pearl is very sweet and cuddly, but she also licks her bum to clean it."

Nia pulled a face. "OK," she said.

"Also, cats do like milk, but they should only have it as a special treat," Mum said. "It can upset their tummies. They should just have it every now and again, like we have ice cream as a treat."

"OK," Nia said, gently pushing Pearl away as she tried to get to her breakfast again. She had so much to learn. They should do lessons about animals at school instead of boring old maths!

"Right, come here, let me sort your hair out, then we'll go." Mum said.

Nia pouted. She really didn't want to leave Pearl when Granny and Kayla got to stay at home with her all day. She stood up so Mum could do her hair.

"There's one good thing about going to school today," Mum said with a grin, as she fiddled with Nia's braids, her fingers twisting and tugging as she neatened all the little plaits and tied them in a ponytail with a bright bobble.

"Ow! What?" Nia said grumpily.

"You get to tell Charlotte all about your new kitten!" Mum laughed. "You can even invite her to stay for dinner tonight if her mum says it's OK. There! All done."

"Thanks!" Nia brightened when she thought about her best friend. Charlotte was going to be so excited!

Nia heard a funny sound coming from the sofa. She turned around and saw Pearl with her head in the cereal bowl. She was lapping at the leftover milk! "Pearl, no!" Nia cried.

Mum rolled her eyes. "How did you pick the most troublesome cat ever?"

Pearl blinked up at them, her eyes wide as if she was saying, "Who, me?" Then she licked her lips and started washing her paws.

Nia giggled. Pearl might be naughty, but she was so much fun!

Nia didn't see Charlotte until after the first bell had rung. Their first lesson today was drama, and Nia was already changing into a black top and trousers when Charlotte arrived.

"Where have you been?" Nia asked. She was bursting to tell her about Pearl!

"We got stuck in a traffic jam behind a tractor," Charlotte said, fiddling with her straight brown hair. "It was going sooo slowly!"

"No chit-chat," Miss Roche said, clapping her hands. "Everyone finish getting changed and get into a circle!"

"I've got amazing news!" Nia whispered, bending down and pretending to tie her shoes.

"What?" Charlotte asked, crouching down next to her.

"I've got a kitten!" Nia said. Her best friend looked amazed, her blue eyes almost as big as Pearl's!

"It's true, we got her yesterday," she said.

"You didn't tell me you were getting one!" Charlotte said, sounding a bit cross.

"I didn't know!" Nia told her.

"I can't believe you've got a kitten!" Charlotte gasped. "What does she look like?"

Nia looked round to check Miss Roche wasn't anywhere near, then showed Charlotte some pictures on her phone that she'd taken last night. Charlotte squealed out loud.

"Shhhh!" Nia hushed, hiding her phone as Miss Roche walked past. They both giggled.

"She's called Pearl and she's only this big." Nia stretched out her hands to show Charlotte how little the kitten was.

"What type is she?" Jade said from behind them.

"Type?" Nia asked.

"What breed is she?" Jade said. "My cat's a Persian. Her official name is Snowflake Duchess Tippytoes, but we call her Snowflake for short."

"Oh. Umm." Nia didn't know how to answer. She didn't know what type Pearl was – she was just a lovely cat!

"What does she look like?" Jade asked impatiently.

"She's really fluffy. She's mainly grey, but

she's got a white tummy. . ." Nia started to say, thinking about Pearl's little pink nose and cute tufty ears. She showed Jade the picture on her phone proudly. But Jade didn't squeal like Charlotte had. Instead she wrinkled her face up like she'd smelled something bad.

"Oh, she's a moggy," Jade said, pushing her glasses up her nose.

"What's a moggy?" Charlotte asked.

"It's a cat that's a mixture, not a pedigree cat," Jade said meanly. "She looks like she might be a bit Persian, because she's so fluffy, but she's not a pedigree."

"She's *perfect*," Nia told her, putting her phone away. She couldn't believe anyone could be horrible about a beautiful little kitten! "She's better than your snooty old cat, anyway." she said under her breath.

Jade didn't hear. "You can't take her to cat shows, because she isn't a pedigree," she continued. "Snowflake's mum won loads of awards and so did her dad. I'm taking Snowflake to the Supreme Cat Show next month, and she's going to win loads too!"

"I could take Pearl to a cat show!" Nia protested.

"No, you couldn't," Jade said, putting her hands on her hips.

"Yes, I could!" Nia shouted.

"Hey, what's all this?" their drama teacher called as she came over. "Dorothy and the Lion are meant to be friends! Now, Jade, come over here. We need to practise your first scene."

As Miss Roche led Jade away, Nia turned to Charlotte.

"Don't listen to her," Charlotte said.

"Don't worry, I don't care what she thinks," Nia said airily. "Pearl is perfect – and I can't wait for you to meet her!"

"Pearl!" Nia ran in the front door and dumped her bags on the floor. She'd been thinking about her kitten all day long, wondering what she was up to. She kept wishing she could phone her and ask what she was doing!

Charlotte had come home with her as usual, and Nia couldn't wait to show her kitten off.

"We have to keep her inside for a while yet," Nia said as they rushed over to the lounge, "until she's had her injections, and then we can let her into the garden."

She opened the lounge door, expecting

the little kitten to be waiting on the other side.

"Pearl!" she called again, looking around the room. But there was no sign of her little cat anywhere. Nia started to feel worried as she looked under the sofas and all around the cat basket. Where could she be?

"My nan's cat, Hector, goes under the TV stand," Charlotte said, crouching down to look. But Pearl wasn't there either.

Nia started to feel panicky.

"Mum!" she shouted. "I can't find Pearl! I think she's got out of the lounge again."

Mum came rushing in. "Don't worry. The door was shut, she must be in here somewhere! There are lots of places a kitten could hide."

They looked all around the sofas and on the bookcases, but there was no sign of Pearl anywhere.

"Even if she has got out of here, she'll still be in the house somewhere," Mum said.

They ran round the house, calling for her. Mum got the box of cat treats and shook it. But Pearl wasn't in the kitchen, or up in any of the bedrooms. Nia felt like she was about to burst into tears. What if Pearl was hurt or lost for ever? She was a brave little cat, but she was so tiny – what if she'd got into real trouble this time?

"Go and get my phone and we'll call Granny and see when she last saw her," Mum said. She rubbed Nia's back reassuringly, but Nia could see she was getting worried too.

Nia hurried back into the lounge. She'd just picked up the phone when she heard a funny *chirp* noise, a bit like a bird.

She looked up and gasped.

"Pearl!" Nia exclaimed. Her naughty little kitten was sitting at the top of the curtains!

"Mum! Charlotte!" Nia yelled in relief. "She's here!"

Mum and Charlotte came running. They both burst out laughing when they saw Pearl perched at the top of the curtains, like a queen looking down at them.

"You silly cat, you scared the life out of me! How did you get all the way up there?" Mum said, half scolding, half laughing. "She must have climbed up and not been able to get down again!"

Mum stood on a chair and carefully brought her down. Pearl didn't seem upset at all.

As Mum gave Pearl a cuddle, Nia stroked her fluffy fur, feeling so relieved. "I thought you were lost!" she said.

"She's absolutely fine, aren't you, troublemaker?" Mum said, planting a kiss on Pearl's tiny head.

"Ohmygosh, she's so gorgeous!" Charlotte gasped. Nia grinned.

"You girls play with her while I make

dinner," Mum said, putting her down on the carpet.

Pearl shook her fur crossly, then looked back up at the curtains.

"Oh, no you don't!" Nia laughed, picking her back up. "Can I take her up to my room?"

"OK, but just for a little while," Mum said. "I don't want any kitten accidents."

"Come on," Nia said to Charlotte.

The girls went upstairs, Nia holding Pearl carefully. As they walked, Nia told Charlotte all about how Pearl had woken her up this morning.

When they got upstairs, Charlotte closed Nia's bedroom door firmly, and Nia sat on the bed with Pearl. Her room was painted white, but she had pink furniture and bedding and a fluffy pink rug over her white-painted floorboards. Charlotte sat opposite her on the bed, with Pearl in the middle. The kitten started exploring around their legs. Charlotte giggled as Pearl's whiskers tickled her toes. She wriggled them and Pearl batted them with her paw.

"She is the cutest thing I've ever seen," she said. "You're so lucky."

"I know," Nia said, smiling at Pearl, who was trying to eat the pom-pom hanging off Charlotte's sock.

"Stop that, naughty!" She picked Pearl up and put her on her lap, running her fingers through her soft fur. Pearl turned around in a circle, then flopped down.

"Are you quite comfortable?" Nia asked her. Pearl looked up and gave a sweet little "miaow!"

Nia and Charlotte both burst out laughing. "I think that means yes," Nia said. "That was the first time I've heard her miaow!"

"My nan told me cats only miaow to us humans," Charlotte said. "They talk to each other using their tails and body language and smells, but they only miaow when they want our attention."

"So she really was talking to me?" Nia said in amazement.

"I guess so!" Charlotte said with a laugh.

Nia looked down at the little grey kitten and felt her heart fill with love.

"I don't care what Jade says, I think she could win any cat competition," Charlotte said.

Pearl looked up, her green eyes wide, and then started a deep rumbling purr of happiness.

"Awwww," both girls squealed.

"That's it – let's put her in the cat show that Jade mentioned!" Charlotte said.

"What?" Nia said.

"You're right – she's the most beautiful

kitten I've ever seen. I bet she could do well in a competition. If you enter her, you could show Jade and her cat Snowflake Snootyface the third!"

Charlotte got up off the bed and started walking about Nia's bedroom, making a plan.

"We need to find out where the cat show is, and if you really have to be a pedigree to enter it," Charlotte said, pacing up and down.

Pearl jumped up and trotted to the end of the bed, watching as Charlotte strode back and forth.

The little cat started peering over the edge of the bed. "Do you want to get down?" Nia asked. But before she could move, Pearl leapt off the end.

"Pearl!" Nia cried, but Pearl was fine. She crouched down, staring at Charlotte's feet.

"What do you want, trouble?" Charlotte said.

Nia burst into giggles. "It's your socks! The pom-poms!"

Charlotte laughed too, and started walking up and down again. Pearl darted towards her, batted a pom-pom with her paw and then raced away.

Nia picked up the little kitten and gave her a cuddle. They were going to enter Pearl in the cat competition – if they could get her to behave for long enough!

"Mum, can we use the computer?" Nia said as they went back downstairs into the lounge. Mum was sitting on the sofa, and Kayla was playing with her toys on the floor.

"Sure, but I thought you'd be playing with Pearl all evening." Mum said in surprise. "You can't be tired of her already."

"It's *for* Pearl," Nia said, putting Pearl down. The little cat went over to her food bowl and sniffed her basket, then raced over to Kayla.

"Tat!" Kayla said, pointing her chubby toddler finger.

"That's Pearl, say Pearl," Nia told her.

"Url," Kayla said, giving a big smile.

"Almost!" Nia bent to give her a kiss on the head.

Mum passed Nia the laptop, and Nia looked up the cat show. "Oh, it's in Birmingham," she said. "Where's Birmingham?"

"It's a couple of hours drive, love. What's in Birmingham?" Mum asked.

"This cat show. A girl called Jade at school takes her cat, and I thought we could take Pearl," Nia said, looking at the website. There were row after row of fancy-looking cats.

"It's way too far, Nia. Besides," Mum jumped up to pick up Pearl, who had climbed up on to Kayla's shoulder and was sniffing Kayla's head while she laughed delightedly. "We can't keep her out of trouble for two minutes, let alone a two-hour car ride!"

"Don't worry," Charlotte said loyally. "We'll find some other way to show Jade that Pearl is the best."

5

"Pearl Madaki," the vet called out.

Nia giggled. She'd never thought about Pearl having her surname. She was sitting in the vet's waiting room, with Pearl in her carrier on her lap. She'd been living with them for eight weeks, and Nia had loved every minute. She was allowed all around the house now, and when Mum opened her door to wake Nia up in the morning, Pearl bounded in, jumping on to the bed for a good morning stroke. Mum made Nia keep her bedroom door shut at night, because Pearl had kept coming and jumping on her all night. Nia loved the idea of going to sleep curled up with her little kitten – but Pearl wouldn't stay still and go to sleep, she wanted to play!

Today they'd brought her to the vets to have all the treatments she needed before she was allowed to go outside. Pearl miaowed at Nia, and Nia put her fingers through the mesh of the cage to stroke her fur reassuringly.

Mum stood up and helped Nia with the basket. The vet was a tall lady with short golden-blonde hair. "I'm Dr Bennett," she said, as she led them into the treatment room. "Aw, she's so gorgeous. Is she yours?" she asked Nia as she looked into the carrier.

Nia nodded proudly.

The vet put the carrier on the table in the middle of the treatment room, and opened the door. But Pearl cowered at the back of the carrier.

"It's OK, Pearl," Nia said, patting the table. "Come on."

Pearl cautiously went towards Nia's voice.

"She's lovely!" the vet said. "So, we need to weigh her and give her a general check over, and then we'll microchip her and give her all the injections she needs, and then she'll have a little operation to make sure she doesn't have lots of kittens."

"Oh," Nia glanced at her mum. She didn't know Pearl was going to have an operation. Besides, she didn't mind if Pearl did have lots of kittens one day, especially if they were as gorgeous as she was!

Mum must have known what Nia was thinking because she shook her head. "One cat is enough," she said. "Besides, it's all part of being a responsible pet owner."

Nia stroked Pearl worriedly. She was still so tiny and an operation was a bit thing.

"It's a very simple procedure, nothing to worry about," Dr Bennett said.

"Dad and Granny are going to come

and pick her up later, so she'll be home by the time you get back from school," Mum promised.

"You hear that, Pearl? It's just a little procedure." Nia stroked her, trying to sound more calm than she felt. But the little kitten didn't seem worried, she was looking around the clinic with interest, her green eyes bright.

"Do you know what a microchip is?" the vet asked.

Nia shook her head.

It's a tiny little plastic chip like a barcode that we put under the fur at the back of their necks," the vet explained. "It doesn't hurt them at all, and it means that if she ever gets lost, we'll be able to scan her chip and find out where you live, and bring her safely back home to you."

Nia nodded, running her fingers through Pearl's soft fur.

"Not that she's going to get lost," Dr Bennett continued. "Right, do you want to pop her on the scales?"

The vet weighed Pearl, listened to her heart, and checked her teeth, typing all the measurements into the computer. "She's perfect!" she said, stroking her between the ears. "Have you got a brush for her? She's gorgeous, with all this beautiful fur, but it means that she'll take a bit more looking after than a shorthair cat."

"I think we need to get one," Mum said.

"We sell them here," the vet told her. "Because she's just a kitten she isn't really going to get knots in her fur yet, but it's really important that you start to groom her now so that she gets used to it for when she's older. When cats have long hair it can get twisted up into what we call a matt. If they don't get groomed it can be painful for them. Shall I show you how to groom her?"

"Yes, please!" Nia said.

Dr Bennett grabbed a brush out of a drawer. "You have to brush them all over, but the main places they get matted is the fur behind their ears and on their tummies." She started combing Pearl's fur. Pearl wriggled, but she seemed to like it.

"Be really careful around her face," the vet said, brushing Pearl's head and making her purr happily. "Longhaired cats do groom themselves with their tongues, but it's just harder for them than shorthair cats, so they need a bit of help."

"That's why cats' tongues are so rough – they're like hairbrushes!" Mum laughed.

Nia nodded. She couldn't wait to groom Pearl properly!

Nia and her mum watched as Dr Bennett quickly gave Pearl the injections for her vaccinations and the microchip in the back of her neck. "Almost done," said Dr Bennett.

"We'll just keep her for the day while we do her op. She'll be home safe and sound by bedtime!"

"Right, say goodbye to Pearl," Mum said.

Nia helped Pearl back into her basket and shut the door. "Love you, Pearl. See you later," she said, trying not to feel too sad.

Pearl's little face looked up at her through the basket, looking confused.

"Come on," Mum said, squeezing Nia's shoulder. "No getting upset, she's absolutely fine. And just think of all the naughtiness she'll be able to get up to out in the garden!"

Nia smiled.

"Let's go and choose her a nice brush," Mum said.

Nia blew Pearl a kiss, then went back out into the reception.

She could hear a sad little meow as she left the room. *It's part of being a responsible pet owner,* she thought to herself, but her tummy was already wriggling with worry. She hated leaving Pearl behind.

Out in the reception, she and Mum looked at the cat brushes. There were lots of different shapes. They found a comb like the one the vet had used, and a brush with a pink handle.

As Mum and the receptionist chatted, Nia looked around the room. There was a big noticeboard with all kinds of advice about dogs and cats, an advert about a rabbit hutch that was for sale, and a notice about the village summer fete.

Nia stepped closer to read it.

We love our pets! This year's annual Village Summer Fete will be animal themed. Do you have the prettiest pup in the village, or the cleverest cat? Join us for all kinds of animal antics on Sunday 3rd July!

On the village green: Dashing Dog Show!

In the church hall: Fancy Felines Competition!

Nia gasped as she read about the cat show.

A special cat show kindly hosted by Mrs Miller, three-time winner of the Supreme Cat Show. Not all cats will enjoy being shown, but if you have a kitten that likes the spotlight, or a calm cat that loves cuddles, come and show them off! Cats of all breeds, shapes and sizes welcome!

Mrs Miller is Jade's mum, Nia thought.

Plus cakes, games, bouncy castle and fun for all ages!

"We'd better get you to school." Mum interrupted her thoughts.

"Mum, look!" Nia exclaimed, pointing at the sign. "We can't go to the cat show in Birmingham, but we could go to this one! It's the day after my play."

Mum looked at the leaflet. "So it's in about two month's time – Pearl will be able to go outside and mix with other cats well before then. OK!"

"Really?" Nia squealed.

Mum nodded. "You'd better practise your grooming and make Pearl look her best." She put her arm around Nia and kissed her on the forehead. "We'll show that Jade girl who's got the best cat, after all!"

Nia was so relieved to see Pearl when she got in from school that night. She'd been thinking about her all day and trying not to worry. Granny said the little cat had been asleep a lot of the afternoon but she mewed happily when she saw Nia, and rubbed up against her fingers. Apart from a little shaved patch on her leg and on her tummy, she didn't look like she'd had an operation at all.

"You're such a brave girl," Nia praised her. "Let's get you some dinner."

Pearl ran straight over to her scratching post, standing on her back legs and clawing at the rough fabric. After running to her basket and sniffing it, she went over to her food bowl.

Nia rushed over to feed her, and Pearl gobbled it up hungrily. She didn't seem to mind having been to the vets at all – it had made her very hungry!

"Look what I got for you this morning. I didn't get chance to show you earlier,"

Nia said, showing her the new brush she'd bought. Pearl came over to sniff it.

"Right, cutie, time to try grooming you," Nia said. "The vet said I have to do it lots while you're little so that you enjoy it when you're older."

She picked Pearl up gently and sat down on the sofa with her on her lap. Pearl tried to wriggle away, but Nia stroked her soothingly and the kitten soon settled down. Then Nia grabbed the cat-grooming tools and started combing through her fur just like the vet had showed her, first using the wide end of the comb, then the narrow end, then using the brush.

Lots of fur came out each time she brushed. Mum came in holding a load of washing, and smiled at her. "Look at all that!" she said. "We could make another cat with all that fur!"

"I'm not pulling it out," Nia said worriedly.

"I know, Nia, it's coming out because it's loose. It's meant to come out, and it's better that you comb it out before it gets all knotty, or sheds all over the carpet. Here," Mum passed Nia a soft red blanket with silky ribbon around the edges. "This was one of Kayla's, but it's a bit old and threadbare now. Why don't you see if Pearl will sit on that? If you use it to comb her every time it'll stop her fur getting everywhere."

"OK," Nia said. She shifted her legs to make Pearl move. Pearl stood up grumpily, stretching out her legs and arching her back like a cartoon witch's cat. "Move just for a second, Pearl," Nia told her.

She lay the soft blanket out on her knees. She'd only just got it in place when Pearl jumped on it, pawing the soft material and turning in a circle, then snuggling back down into her lap.

"She likes it!" Nia laughed.

As Nia stroked the comb down Pearl's back, Pearl stretched her paws out and started clawing with one paw after the other.

"Ouch!" Nia said, batting Pearl's paw away from her leg. "Ouch!" she yelped as Pearl did again. "I'm not your scratching post, Pearl!"

Pearl looked up at her and gave a soft meow.

"I don't understand," Nia said to Mum. "She seems so happy, why does she keep clawing me?"

"Let's see," Mum said, coming over. Nia started gently combing the fur behind Pearl's ears and, sure enough, Pearl dug her claws into the blanket again. "See!" Nia cried. "I'm not being rough."

"I think cats do that when they're really happy," Mum said. "I'll look it up." She got out her phone and started typing.

Nia stroked Pearl. She was lolloping on her lap, her eyes half shut, a gentle purring noise rumbling though her tiny body. She certainly seemed happy.

"Yes!" Mum said. "It's called 'milk treading'. Apparently baby kittens do it to their mums when they want to be fed, and grown-up cats do it when they're really, really content. She doesn't know she's hurting you!"

"Aw!" Nia said.

"This can help with that too," Mum said, folding over the silky edge of the blanket and tucking it under Pearl's paws. "Now try."

Now when Pearl started kneading, her claws dug into the silky material.

"That's better," Nia grinned, running the brush all over the kitten's fur.

Pearl started licking her paws as Nia combed her ears. "Good girl," Nia giggled, bending down to kiss her soft head. Pearl looked up at her as if to ask why she'd stopped combing.

"Oh, sorry, Your Highness!" Nia joked, starting to brush again. Maybe Pearl could act like a princess, after all!

6

"I'm the Cowardly Lion," Nia said in her growly lion voice. She was in the bath, surrounded by bubbles, trying to remember her lines for the school play.

"Raaaoow!" She practised her lion roar.

From outside the door there was a "meow" in reply.

"Pearl?" she called.

There was a knock at the door and Mum opened it. "This one was sat outside, pining for you!" she said. Nia giggled as Pearl trotted in. "Hello!" she said. "Did you miss me?"

"Meow," Pearl replied seriously. She

jumped up on to the toilet lid and peered at Nia in the bubbly water.

Nia scooped up some bubbles and held them out to the kitten. Pearl batted them with her paw. Mum and Nia both laughed.

"She is adorable," Mum grinned.

They heard the sound of Kayla crying from her room. "Come on, Pearl," Mum said. "Let's go." She left the bathroom and Pearl followed her.

Nia lay back down and started rehearsing her lines again. But a second later the door creaked open, and Pearl jumped up right on to the side of the bath. "Meow!" she said happily.

"Hello, trouble!" said Nia. "What are you doing back in here?"

Pearl walked down the edge of the bath like she was on a tightrope.

"You be careful, you don't want to fall in," Nia said. She wanted to put Pearl safely down on the floor, but her hands were all wet.

"Mum!" she called. "Be careful," she told Pearl, as the tiny cat reached out to paw at some bubbles.

Mum came back in, holding Kayla, and picked Pearl up. "You're a pest, Pearl," said Mum, taking the nosy kitten back out with her.

Nia smiled as she swooshed around the bubbles. It would have been funny if Pearl had fallen in – but she didn't think the kitten would like it very much.

Just then the door swung open again and Pearl sneaked back in once more.

"You again!" Nia laughed.

"Meow!" Pearl said plaintively.

"We're trying to stop you from getting wet!" Nia told her. "No," Nia said as Pearl jumped up on the toilet lid. "Don't come on the side. NO, Pearl," she said firmly.

Pearl's bum gave that wiggle that meant she was about to pounce.

But this time instead of nimbly jumping on the side, she missed, and slipped right into the bath!

Nia squealed as bubbles and water went everywhere.

Pearl splashed in the water then scrambled out up the side and jumped down on to the bath mat. She shook herself. She looked much smaller and darker with her fur wet. "Meow," she said crossly.

"I told you not to!" Nia gasped.

Mum came back in and burst into laughter. "Well that was bound to happen," she said. "Maybe next time she'll listen to you!"

Pearl looked at them, and then flipped over and started attacking the towel that was dangling off the radiator. Her swim in the bath didn't seem to have taught her a lesson, she was as naughty as ever!

Nia bounced up and down excitedly as the phone rang. Finally Charlotte answered.

"Do you want to come to my house?" Nia asked. "We're going to let Pearl outside for the first time!"

Charlotte squealed so loudly that Mum grinned from across the kitchen. "I guess that's a yes!"

Nia nodded. She glanced under the table to look for Pearl, who was lying under Kayla's high chair. As Nia watched, she grabbed one of the wooden legs with her paws and started scratching it with her back legs.

"No, Pearl!" Granny told her off.

Pearl sat up and looked up at Granny innocently.

Granny chuckled and reached down to stroke Pearl under the chin.

Nia smiled. She played with Pearl a lot, but the little kitten always had so much energy. She was really excited for Pearl to go outside and have adventures out there.

"What time shall I come over?" Charlotte asked.

"Now!" Nia told her.

Charlotte giggled. "I'll ask Mum," she said.

Nia could hear her muffled conversation with her mum.

"OK, be there soon!" Charlotte said.

"Yay! Bye!" Nia hung up the phone and went to pick up Pearl before she started scratching again.

Pearl stretched out in her arms. She was much bigger than she had been when they first got her. Nia thought about the marks Dad made on the kitchen wall to measure her height. They should have done the same thing with Pearl, but measuring how long she was getting. She'd already grown so much!

"Oh, keep hold of her. I've got something for her," Mum said, putting down her tea towel and rushing out of the room.

Nia looked at Pearl and Pearl looked up at her. Nia shrugged. "I don't know what it is either," she said.

Mum came back in with a bag. "Open it!" she said.

Nia sat down. Pearl shuffled about on her lap, but Nia stroked her and she sat down, purring.

Nia opened the bag.

Granny and Mum watched excitedly.

Inside was a purple cat collar. "It's got a quick release clasp so it won't hurt her if she gets it stuck on anything," Mum said, opening and closing the catch. "And look!"

At the front of the collar was a bell and a little silver disk with PEARL written on it. On the back was their telephone number.

"I love it!" Nia exclaimed. "Thanks, Mum. Look, Pearl! It's so pretty, and it's for you!"

Nia showed Pearl the collar. Pearl put out her paw to bat the shiny disk.

"I think that means she likes it!" Nia giggled.

Mum carefully looped the collar around Pearl's neck and adjusted it until it was just right. Pearl wriggled a bit, but once it was on she didn't seem to notice. She looked even cuter than before.

She jumped down off Nia's lap and the bell on the collar rang. Pearl twitched her ears and looked around to see where the sound was coming from.

Nia giggled again.

"She'll get used to the noise," Mum said. "The bell is so that she can't attack all the garden birds – they'll be able to hear her coming."

Pearl took a step forward and her bell rang again. At the same time, the doorbell sounded. "That one wasn't Pearl," Mum joked.

Nia left Pearl still shaking her bell and ran to open the door. Charlotte was there, but so were Dad and Kayla, back from Kayla's swimming class.

"Quick! Come and see what Pearl's got!" Nia said.

Everyone followed Nia in and cooed over Pearl's new collar. "Right, now everyone's here, it's time to let her outside!" Mum said.

Suddenly, Nia didn't feel ready. She felt a ripple of nerves in her tummy. *What if Pearl went out and didn't come back? What if she got lost?*

"Um," Nia said as Mum stared at her.

"What's wrong?" Mum asked. "You were so excited a minute ago!"

"What if she gets lost?" Nia asked worriedly. "She's so small and we can't make her stay in the garden; cats can climb garden fences. What if she goes too far and can't find her way home?"

"She won't." Dad put Kayla down and put his arm around Nia. "She'll probably stick really close to us. We can all go out in the garden and hang out with her. Besides, she'll come in when she's hungry, look!" He picked up a box of cat treats and shook it. Pearl came rushing over to him.

"Miaow!" she said, standing up on her back legs to claw at Dad's trousers.

Dad laughed and gave her a treat.

"Besides, you can't keep her in for ever, Nia," Mum said. "She's got a happy home here; I promise she'll come back."

Pearl trotted away from Dad and jumped

up at the kitchen windowsill, looking outside. Her ears twitched, and she made the funny growly chirping noise she made when she saw a bird. Nia knew she would love being able to run around in the garden. She took a deep breath and nodded. "OK!"

Dad unlocked the cat flap and Pearl went over to see what he was doing.

Charlotte squeezed Nia's hand.

Pearl looked at the cat flap. Dad pushed it open. "Look out there," he said, but Pearl just sat down and looked up at him.

"I think we might have to train her how to use the cat flap!" Mum said. "Open the back door for now."

Mum got her phone out to film it, and Dad opened the back door. Nia held her breath – but Pearl just sat there. She sat in the doorway, looking outside, curious, but not moving.

"Go on, Pearl," Nia said softly. Pearl turned

at the sound of her voice, then ran and sat next to her legs. "You're meant to be going outside, not further inside!" Nia laughed.

"Why don't you go outside and call her?" Mum suggested. "She might follow you."

Nia and Charlotte went out into the garden. Mum came out too and spread a blanket on the grass. It was a bright sunny day, with just a few cotton-ball white clouds in the blue sky, and the sun was warm on Nia's shoulders. But she couldn't take her eyes off Pearl. As she and Charlotte sat and watched from the blanket, Pearl edged closer to the door.

"Pearl!" Nia called, shaking the cat treats.

"Meow," Pearl replied from the doorway.

"It's OK, it's safe," Nia told her.

Pearl sniffed all around the door frame, then put one paw, then two, over the doorstep. Her front paws were out but her body was still inside.

The girls watched, giggling at the little kitten. She was normally so brave, but being outside was a big new thing for her.

Finally she stepped out of the doorway and started sniffing around the plant pots and flower beds. She stepped tentatively on to the grass, lifting her paws high as she came over to Nia, as if the grass was tickling her paws. "You're so cute," Nia said, giving her a stroke and a treat.

"Keep an eye on her," Mum said, "but I don't think she'll go too far."

Nia and Charlotte lay on their tummies in the sunshine, lazily watching as Pearl explored the garden.

"Did you hear about the cat show?" Nia asked Charlotte.

"In Birmingham?" Charlotte said.

"No, there's going to be one here!" Nia explained about the summer fete. "We're going to take Pearl!"

"She'll win for sure," Charlotte said loyally.

Nia grinned. She knew Charlotte was being nice, but she honestly thought Pearl might win – after all, what could be better than her gorgeous little kitten?

The girls lolled around in the sunshine. They did handstands and made daisy chains and practised their lines for the play, all the time looking to see where Pearl was.

"Wasn't Jade annoying in drama yesterday?" Charlotte said, rolling her eyes.

"I know!" Nia exclaimed. Their show was in a week and Jade was being more of a pain than ever. The drama teacher kept making Jade, Nia and Jenny and Parvi, who were playing Dorothy's other friends the Tin Man and the Scarecrow, link arms as they walked around. Jade kept pulling Nia's arm so that she lost her balance and almost fell over. Even worse, Jade kept boasting about how *she* was the star of the whole play.

"Mum says just ignore her," Nia said, rolling over and watching Pearl as she scratched her claws on a tree. A butterfly darted among the lavender bushes and the little cat stared at it in amazement.

"Just think – a couple more weeks and it's the play, and then it's the holidays and we can do this all summer!" Charlotte said.

Pearl came over to the girls, purring, and flopped down on the grass beside them.

Nia reached out to stroke her pet, but the kitten's usually soft fur felt funny. Nia sat up to look at her properly. Pearl flipped over on to her back, thinking she was going to get a tickle on her tummy.

"Turn over, silly, and let me look at you!" Nia said. She picked Pearl up and put her on her lap. Her fur was so dirty! It was streaked with mud, and her coat was covered with bits of grit and dirt.

"Oh, Pearl!" she cried. "You're so dirty!"

Pearl was going to need lots of grooming – and maybe another dip in the bath!

Granny was helping Nia put her costume on. It was a brown leotard with yellow woollen ruffs around her hands and feet, and a big golden-brown-and-yellow woollen mane around her face. A long tail made from a pair of brown tights, with a tassel of yellow wool at the end, hung down behind her. "I can't wait to see what Kayla and Pearl think!" Nia giggled.

"Hold still!" Granny said, rapping Nia on the nose with a paintbrush. "Otherwise you will not have straight whiskers."

Nia stood as still as she could, even though inside she was hopping up and down with excitement.

She could feel Pearl was rubbing around her legs happily, and Nia wanted to bend down and stroke her, but she didn't want to be told off again. As she waited for Granny to finish, she felt a strange tugging behind her. Pearl was playing with the lion tail!

"Done," Granny said finally. Nia turned around and grabbed her naughty kitten. "Stop pulling my tail, Pearl," she scolded jokingly. "I don't pull your tail, so don't pull mine!" Then she ran over to the mirror. The tip of her nose was painted pink and she had long black whiskers on her cheeks. Gold and yellow lines fanned out on her forehead to make her eyebrows look big and bushy like her mane. She looked just like a lion!

She squealed in delight and hugged Granny. "Thank you!"

"What do you think, Pearl?" she asked, holding her kitten up to her face.

Pearl looked at her for a second, then bumped her head against Nia's chin. "Aw, you love me even when I'm a lion," Nia said.

"Come, we must show Kayla," Granny said.

"Oh yes!" Nia grinned as they raced downstairs.

Kayla was in her high chair dressed in a pretty red velvet dress, all ready for Nia's show.

Nia put Pearl down and she padded into the kitchen.

Nia dropped down on to all fours and followed behind her, doing her best lion walk, her shoulders slinking forward and her tail swishing behind her.

At first, Kayla didn't see her, but then she burst out laughing.

"Funny Nia," she said.

"Oh," Nia pretended to be disappointed. "I didn't even convince Kayla I was a cat!"

"You're going to be great!" Mum said, picking up Kayla. "And we'll all be there cheering for you. Except Pearl, but she'll be cheering from home."

Nia looked at Pearl, and she gave one of her birdy *chirps*. Nia giggled. Maybe that meant "good luck!"

As they drove to school, Nia started to feel nervous. She recited her first lines over and over in her head. It was strange going into school in the evening. The playground was full of parents' cars, and there were mums and dads and brothers and sisters everywhere.

"You'd better go backstage while we find a seat," Mum said.

"Good luck!" Granny said, giving her a tight squeeze.

"You're going to be brilliant," Dad said, kissing the top of her head.

Nia put her tail over her arm and ran

across the playground to the back of the school hall. She saw Charlotte straight away. She looked fantastic, with bright green face paint, a crooked nose, straggly hair made out of a black bin bag, and a black dress and broom.

"Nia!" Charlotte squealed, sounding very unwitchy. "I'm SO nervous!"

Nia held her hand tight. "It's OK, we can do it," she said although her heart was pounding. The two girls linked arms and ran inside together.

There were people everywhere. It didn't feel like school at all, everything was very strange. Nia felt her nerves get even worse.

"Right everyone, gather round." Miss Roche looked very glamourous with her hair and make-up done. "You've all worked very hard, so now go out there and have fun!"

Jade pranced in. She looked perfect,

with her blonde hair in two long plaits, a blue-and-white gingham dress and sparkly red ruby slippers. "I don't know why you're nervous," she said to Charlotte and Nia spitefully. "It's not like you're the star."

"She's so awful," Charlotte said as Jade flounced away. Nia glanced at her friend and was amazed to see that Charlotte looked as if she was about to cry.

"Don't smudge your face!" Nia said. "We're going to be the best witch and the best lion we can be. Go out there and – think of a spell that will make Jade's nose fall off!"

Charlotte gave a small giggle. "OK!" she said, pulling the pointy hat down on her head firmly.

Nia nodded happily as her friend marched on stage, cackling loudly.

She peered through the thick, heavy curtain at all the faces in the audience and felt a bit sick. She knew what she'd told Charlotte was true ... but suddenly she didn't feel so brave.

Nia stood at the side of the stage. Out onstage, Jade was talking loudly and clearly. She didn't look nervous at all.

Charlotte said her last line in that scene and ran off stage cackling loudly. The audience all booed and clapped.

"That was so much fun!" Charlotte gasped as she raced to Nia's side.

Nia felt so nervous all she could do was nod.

"Nia!" Miss Roche prompted, nodding at the stage. It was her turn to go on.

Nia froze.

"Go on!" Miss Roche urged.

Nia's knees felt weak. She couldn't remember her lines!

"What's wrong?" Charlotte asked.

"I can't do it!" Nia whispered back, feeling like she was about to burst into tears.

"Yes you can!" Charlotte gave Nia's hand a reassuring squeeze. "Think about Pearl; she's so small but so adventurous. If she can do it, you can too."

Nia thought about Pearl and felt a tiny bit better.

"Nia!" Miss Roche was getting impatient. "Go ON!"

But Nia was still thinking. She didn't know how to be a lion ... but she did know how to be a cat – a cat like Pearl.

She dropped to her knees and started to crawl onstage, doing her funny shoulder walk.

The audience laughed – they loved it!

Nia felt warm inside. She looked out into the crowd and spotted her family, sitting near the front. Mum was waving and Kayla was pointing a chubby finger at her. Granny was jigging up and down with excitement. Dad gave her a thumbs up. Nia crawled all the way over to Jade. Her confused face almost made Nia giggle.

When Jade started talking, Nia remembered all her lines. But she couldn't stop pretending to be like Pearl – she knew why the little cat was naughty, it was so much fun!

As Jade was saying her next lines, Nia stole a pie out of her basket and pretended to eat it. When Jade turned around to see why the audience were laughing, Nia started pretending to lick her paws. The audience roared with laughter!

Jade looked at her crossly, but Nia didn't care. Whenever Jade glanced her way, she stopped being naughty and looked up at her with big eyes, just like Pearl.

The best bit was when Charlotte came back on, being the witch. Nia had to be scared. In rehearsals, she'd just put her paws to her mouth, but today she bounded to the edge of the stage and pretend to climb up the curtains, just like Pearl had.

Unlike Jade, who was looking crosser and crosser, Charlotte loved the way Nia was acting. "Get down here, you silly lion!" she improvised, in her witchiest voice. "Before I turn you into a rug for my castle! Mwa ha ha ha!" Charlotte cackled and the audience cheered.

The whole play was really fun. A few things went wrong: Nia's tail fell off and Charlotte forgot some of her lines, but no one seemed to mind.

When Nia ran off stage at the end, Miss Roche gave her a hug. "That was just wonderful, Nia," she said. "At the start I thought you weren't even going to go on, but you were excellent! You're going to be a brilliant actress one day."

"Real actresses don't get stage fright," Nia said, feeling her happiness fade away.

"Yes they do!" Miss Roche said, looking into Nia's eyes seriously. "But then they do exactly what you did – they go on stage anyway and act their socks off!"

She gave Nia's shoulder a squeeze. "Now come on, everyone – onstage for a bow!"

She led them all onstage. They stood in a big line, Nia holding Charlotte and Jade's hands. As each of them stepped forward like they'd practised, the audience clapped and cheered. But Nia got the biggest cheer of all, even bigger than Jade's. The audience sprang to their feet. Nia looked at her family who were clapping and whistling and grinning.

Out in the playground afterwards, Dad picked her up and swung her around. "I'm so proud of you!" he said. "I told you, be the best lion you can be, and look what happened! You don't have to be *the* star to be a star."

Nia beamed with pride. It had been the best play ever – and it was all thanks to Pearl!

"We'd better go home and give Pearl a brush," Mum reminded her. "After all, you're not the only star in the family. We need to get her looking beautiful for the pet show tomorrow!"

"Better put your wellies on," Mum said as she looked out of the window on the morning of the fete. "We're having a proper British summer – it's very wet!"

Nia ran over to see outside. Her heart sank as she saw the rain splashing down into the puddles.

"Can we still go?" she asked.

"Of course," Mum said. "It's inside, anyway."

When they got to the village green, Nia gasped – it looked so different! It was normally a big patch of grass where people walked their dogs or played games, but today it was covered in big white marquee tents, and there were people everywhere.

"A bit of rain won't stop us having fun!" A man with a big loudspeaker was calling out as they hurried across the field, carrying Pearl in her cat basket. "The vegetable contest is taking place at three p.m. As you know, today is all about the animals, so this year we're doing an animal vegetable contest!" the man continued. "Have you made a collie dog out of a cauliflower? Or a bunny out of broccoli? We want to see your crazy animal veg sculptures! All entrants for the animal veg competition, please go to tent number two!"

Nia giggled at the idea of vegetable animal sculptures. "The cat show is in the church hall," Mum said, leading them over.

The church hall looked different too. Pretty bunting was looped from the ceiling. The usual piles of stacked-up chairs and the refreshment table were missing, and in their place long tables were laid out all along the length of the hall. On top of the tables were lots of animal pens, and in each one of those was a different cat! Nia had no idea there were so many cats in her village!

She walked down the lines of tables, peering at all the cats. The lady from the bakery had two little black-and-white cats. A few people from Nia's school were there with their pets, and even Miss Roche the drama teacher was fussing around a big ginger cat in her pen.

Some of the cats were meowing, but some were sitting quietly. Nia looked at each one carefully as she passed. None of them were as cute as Pearl!

Pearl was shifting around in her basket, making it hard to carry. "Nearly there, Pearl," Nia soothed her.

"Here's our spot," Mum said, showing them to an empty pen at the end of the line. Mum started getting out their supplies. They'd been told to bring a litter tray, and food and water bowls with them, as well as a cushion or something cosy for the cats to lie on. Nia had brought the red blanket and her brush to make sure Pearl looked perfect before she went in front of the judges.

Mum helped put Pearl inside the pen, and set out the litter tray and food bowls. Pearl sniffed them all interestedly, then sat staring out of the cage at all the other cats nearby.

"Meow," she said curiously.

"It's OK," said Nia. She got out the comb and started brushing Pearl's fur. The little grey kitten looked around once more, then sat down, purring happily. She didn't mind the fuss at all.

"Nia!" Charlotte came running over. "I've never seen so many cats!" she said. "But Pearl is definitely the best."

"Thanks!" Nia giggled at her friend's enthusiasm.

"I wanted Nan to bring her cat, Hector," Charlotte said, "but she said he'd hate it. She said he'd probably scratch the judge!"

Nia laughed, then stopped when she heard a familiar – and annoying – voice. Jade!

Jade was standing next to a tall woman that Nia guessed was her mum. The woman had blonde hair that was almost as big and curly as that of the big white cat she was holding. It was beautiful, but it was so fluffy that Nia could barely see its eyes, and it had a miserable look on its face.

Dr Bennett the vet came over, wearing a badge that read JUDGE.

"Dr Bennett," Jade's mum drawled. "So

glad I could help with your little show. All the equipment came from the biggest cat contest in the country." She waved a long-nailed hand airily at the room. "They know me and Snowflake, of course, and it was no problem for them to lend it to me. Of course, the standard of competitor won't be the same in our little village."

"Well, it's just a little bit of fun," the vet said, tucking her short golden hair behind her ears. "And I think we have some gorgeous cats here today."

"We can't all be champions like my Snowflake," Jade's mum said with a tinkly laugh.

"No wonder Jade's awful if that's what her mum is like!" Mum whispered to Nia.

"Do you want to look round the rest of the fete?" Charlotte asked.

Nia felt torn; she did, but she didn't want to leave Pearl... She glanced at the little kitten who was curled up in her basket with her eyes closed. Her little tummy was going up and down as she slept. Granny and Kayla were looking at a nearby cat, and Dad was talking to its owner.

"Go on," Mum said. "I'll look after her."

"OK!" Nia blew Pearl a kiss. Charlotte grabbed her hand and they ran outside.

The rain had stopped. The ground was muddy, but if it wasn't for that no one would have known it had been raining. The sun was shining and the sky was a beautiful blue. There were happy shrieks and shouts coming from the green in the middle of the village where Nia and Charlotte could see a bouncy castle had been set up. Dotted about were stalls selling candyfloss and ice cream, and everywhere Nia looked there were people with their pets!

In one corner of the field was a big tent. "That's where all the smaller animals are going," Charlotte told her. "Steph is bringing her guinea pig. Let's go and see."

They ran past a fenced-off area, with a large crowd gathered around. Inside, lots of dogs and their owners were lined up. As the girls paused for a second, a squashy-faced pug and his owner went up to collect a ribbon.

"Come on!" Charlotte dragged Nia over to the little animal tent.

Inside were big pens filled with straw with lots of guinea pigs and rabbits snuffling around in them.

"Look, there's Steph," Charlotte said. Steph was holding a black-and-tan guinea pig.

"He's so cute!" Nia told her, stroking the little guinea pig. It made a happy squeaking noise that made the girls giggle.

"Have you seen the baby rabbits?" Steph said. "They're soooooo sweet! Some of them are for sale, I'm going to ask my stepmum if I can have one."

The girls shook their heads. Steph pointed to a pen in the corner.

As they went over, they saw that Charlotte's mum was already there. "Hi, Mum!" Charlotte said.

"Oh, Lottie, you're going to love these!" her mum said. She moved over so the girls could stand next to her and look into the pen. It was filled with lots of tiny bunnies with floppy ears. "Aren't they adorable!" Charlotte's mum said.

"They're so cute!" Charlotte squealed. The girls watched as one nibbled a chunk of carrot.

"I think it's been really good for you to have a pet, Nia," Charlotte said in a loud voice, like she was back onstage, doing the play.

"What?" Nia asked, feeling confused.

Charlotte nudged her arm and nodded her head at her mum. "Don't you think having Pearl has been a brilliant thing?"

"Oh, YES," Nia replied loudly as she understood what her friend was doing. "Mum says I'm much more organized and responsible now that I have a pet."

"Oh, really?" Charlotte replied. "It's very good for kids our age to have a pet, isn't it?"

"Definitely," Nia replied.

"I know what you're up to, girls!" Charlotte's mum said, with a shake of her head.

Charlotte giggled, but Nia didn't. Suddenly she was desperate for her best friend to have a pet. She couldn't imagine not having Pearl – the thought made her heart hurt.

"Honestly," she said to Charlotte's mum, "I love Pearl. And sometimes I don't want to help Mum clean out the stinky litter tray, or I can't be bothered to brush her, but I always do, because I have to look after her, because I love her. And I'm SO lucky to have her." She looked at Charlotte's mum earnestly.

Charlotte's mum laughed and gave her a gentle hug. "Aw, that's lovely, Nia. I will think about it, OK?"

"OK!" Nia replied.

There was a crackly sound of the loudspeaker, and a voice boomed across the green. "Ladies and gentlemen, boys and girls, would all competitors for the cat show make their way to the church hall. The judging will start in five minutes."

"Now you'd better head over to the church hall and make sure that beautiful kitten of yours wins!" Charlotte's mum said.

Nia and Charlotte grabbed hands and ran towards the hall. It was show time – again!

9

The girls ran to the hall and wove through all the people back to where Nia's family were waiting with Pearl. Dr Bennett went up to the little stage at the end of the hall. She tapped on the microphone that was set up there, and the noise bounced around the hall.

"Hello, everyone!" she said, her voice booming out. "And welcome to the first ever cat show at our village fete. I'm hoping it'll be such a success that it'll be an annual event. Thank you all for coming, and special thanks to Mrs Miller for organizing."

She nodded at Jade's mum, then looked surprised as Mrs Miller rushed onstage to talk into the microphone, holding Snowflake. She was an even bigger show-off than Jade!

"As well as Dr Bennett," Jade's mum said, "we have a special judge here too. Mr Francis normally judges at big cat shows, but he's made a special trip as a personal favour to me." She gave a sickly-sweet smile as the judge came on stage. He was short and round, with a long ponytail hanging down his back and a pair of glasses perched on the end of his nose. He nodded his head as everyone clapped, but he didn't smile at all.

Dr Bennett finally took back the microphone. "Right, on with the show! There will be several *cat*-agories," she said, pausing as everyone groaned. "And I hope you're all *feline* lucky today. One at a time, bring your cat up to the judging table for us to examine. We know this isn't a pedigree cat show, and I personally happen to prefer the beautiful range of house cats we have here, whether they're ginger toms or black-and-white moggies. We're not looking for pedigree or breeding here today..."

Jade's mum pulled a face.

"... We'll be looking for the healthiest coat, the prettiest eyes and, of course, the cat with the best *purr*sonality. May the best cats win!" Dr Bennett finished with a big grin.

One by one, each competitor brought their cat up to the judging table. The judges gave the cats a stroke, checked their teeth and paws, and made lots of notes.

"Of course, at a *real* cat show this would be much more detailed," Nia overheard Jade's mum saying. All the other cats were in their pens, but she was still carrying Snowflake around draped half over her shoulder, like she was a fancy scarf.

"Next we have Nia and her cat, Pearl," the vet called. Nia felt a buzz of nerves, but then she looked at Pearl, who was watching everything with interest. She wasn't nervous – so Nia wouldn't be either! Nia opened Pearl's pen. "Now, be good," she whispered. She picked Pearl up and carefully took her over to the stand.

For a minute, everything went well. Pearl sat perfectly still, looking up at the judges with her big eyes, as they stroked her. But then, something caught her attention, and she started staring at Mr Francis.

Nia looked from her kitten to the judge in confusion. As he moved, she saw his ponytail hanging down – just like her lion tail, or Pearl's favourite dangling cat toy...

Oh no! Nia thought.

As Mr Francis moved again and his hair swished, Pearl's ears went back and her bum gave a wriggle. Nia knew what that meant – she was going to pounce.

"No, Pearl," Nia muttered.

Pearl looked at her and gave a plaintive meow.

"No!" Nia said again.

But it was too late. As Mr Francis moved again, Pearl jumped up on to his arm.

"Pearl!" Nia cried out as the naughty cat climbed up the judge's arm and over his shoulder, reaching out her little paws, trying to catch his hair!

Everyone else in the tent was laughing, but Mr Francis's face was going very red. It didn't look like he was finding it funny at all.

Just then, Nia had an idea. While the judges tried to unhook Pearl's claws, she ran back to their pen and came back holding the red blanket.

Nia spread it out on the judges' table. "Pearl," she called, patting it.

Pearl leapt straight off the Mr Francis' back and on to the table. Then she sat there, her paws neatly together, looking up at both judges innocently.

This made everyone laugh even more. Dr Bennett was red with trying to hold in her laughter. Everyone was laughing apart from Jade's mum and Mr Francis.

"That cat should be disqualified!" Jade's mum said loudly, coming over to console Mr Francis, still carrying Snowflake.

Nia felt her face going hot. "I don't care if you are disqualified," she whispered to Pearl. "No matter what anyone else says, I know you're the best," she said, kissing the kitten on the top of her fluffy head.

She glanced up and Mrs Miller shot her a mean look as she leaned over Mr Francis, with Snowflake still in her arms.

But as Nia watched, Snowflake Duchess Tippytoes sprang off of Mrs Miller's shoulder – and attacked the judge's hair too!

"Snowflake, get down this instant!" Jade's mum bellowed, trying to peel Snowflake off the judge. "Oh, Mr Francis, I'm so sorry, Snowflake has never acted like this before!" she said. She snatched up the big fluffy cat, which gave a cross yowl.

"Still think that they should be disqualified?" Dr Bennett asked wryly.

"Well no … a simple accident … that cat led Snowflake astray!" Mrs Miller said, pointing at Pearl.

Mr Francis was going redder and redder – and then he burst out laughing. As he gave a big belly chuckle everyone else laughed too.

Nia stroked Pearl's ears. She was washing her paws, as if she had no idea about the trouble she'd caused.

"I think that's enough from Pearl," Dr Bennett laughed.

Nia picked up Pearl and went back to her pen. Her family all crowded round to give Pearl a stroke.

"Shall we go home?" Nia asked.

"They need to announce the winners first," Dad said.

"Well Pearl hasn't won anything!" Nia said.

"You never know," Dad told her, giving her a squeeze.

The prizes were given out, and everyone clapped politely. Nia couldn't clap because she was holding Pearl. The naughty kitten was now being perfectly behaved, snuggled up cosily in Nia's arms.

One by one the awards were given out and Pearl didn't win – but neither did Snowflake, and Jade's mum was looking crosser and crosser each time someone went up to get a ribbon.

Finally, Dr Bennett held out a big purple ribbon that read WINNER in big letters.

"There'd no doubt that one cat here deserves the prize for best *purr*sonality. She might be small, but she's a huge character. With an unanimous decision, we'd like to award this prize to ... Pearl!"

"Pearl!" Nia gasped in amazement at hearing her pet's name. She glanced at her mum, who nodded happily.

Nia walked up to the stage, feeling like she was in a dream. She held Pearl tightly as Mr Francis came near, but Pearl was too sleepy to be naughty.

Mr Francis gave Pearl a stroke. Then he handed Nia the big purple ribbon.

"Congratulations, she's a lovely little cat," he said. "I'm sure she'll be lots of fun. And she's beautifully groomed; you're obviously a very good owner."

Nia felt herself get hot again – but this

time it was with pride. "Thank you," she said. "Um, I'm sorry about your hair."

He laughed. "It's OK, it's a natural instinct for a cat," he said. "And maybe it is time I had a haircut." As they talked, a photographer came over and waved at him. "We have to pose for a photo with Pearl," Mr Francis told her.

He held the ribbon up in the air above Pearl's head. Nia smiled at the photographer, but as she did, she felt Pearl move. The little kitten had her paws in the air, trying to get the ribbon!

Everyone laughed. The photographer came over and showed them the photos – a perfectly posed one, with Pearl looking up at the ribbon, and in the next, Nia and the judge staring as Pearl attacked it.

"I think I know which one we'll use – the perfect one doesn't show her personality!" The photographer chuckled.

Nia rushed back to her family. Mum put her arm around her and Charlotte, Granny and Kayla cooed over the ribbon.

"You and Pearl *both* stole the show!" Dad said with a grin.

"You both have big *purr*sonalities. You're made for each other!" agreed Mum.

Nia looked down at her kitten. "Yes, we are!"

Charlotte's mum came over as they were putting Pearl back in her carrier.

"We'll drop Pearl at home and then come back and enjoy the rest of the fete while she has a well-earned nap," Dad said. "Unless you think she'd like to go and cause trouble at the dog show?!"

"I think she's had enough adventures for one day," said Nia.

"What's she done now?" Charlotte's mum asked.

They explained. Charlotte's mum laughed.

"But look how lovely she is!" Charlotte said. "And smaller animals are less of a responsibility. Like a tiny, baby rabbit, that wouldn't be much trouble at all..."

She looked at her mum, her eyes as big as Pearl's.

"Those baby rabbits *were* cute," her mum said.

"Oh please, Mum, please can I have one?" Charlotte begged. "I promise I'd feed it and clean it out every day."

"I guess you're old enough to be responsible..." her mum said.

Nia crossed her fingers as Charlotte looked at her mum. "But you'd have to wait until we get a hutch and everything for the garden," Charlotte's mum said.

"Oh thank you, thank you, thank you!" Charlotte squealed. "Nia, come with me and choose one!"

Nia looked down at Pearl, who was

curled up in her cat carrier, her tail around her feet, fast asleep. "OK! I just have to take my prize-winning kitten home first."

"Pearl!" Nia called. "Pearl, come out from under there!"

She'd been doing her homework on her bed, and Pearl had come into her room. But instead of sitting on Nia's lap like she usually did, she'd gone exploring underneath the bed. She was rustling around under there. Nia didn't know what she was doing, but it sounded like she was making a mess!

Nia peered over the edge of her bed. Pearl looked back from where she was curled up on top of a cardboard box. As Nia watched, she tore a piece off the side, then looked up at Nia innocently.

"Come out, you naughty kitten," Nia ordered.

She patted the floor and Pearl crept out. Nia picked her up and put her on the bed, then grabbed the brush and red blanket from her chest of drawers. As she did she grinned at the purple ribbon pinned next to her mirror. It sat alongside a photo of her and Charlotte, holding her new rabbit. Charlotte had chosen a tiny light-brown rabbit with floppy ears and called her Toffee. She was lovely – almost as nice as Pearl, although not quite as interesting.

Just then Nia saw Pearl in the mirror, about to climb back under her bed. "Oh, no you don't!" she laughed. She grabbed Pearl and sat down with the kitten on her lap. As soon as she saw the blanket and the brush, Pearl snuggled down happily. She loved being brushed, and Nia adored doing it. Not because she wanted to make Pearl look fancy for a show, but just because she loved her.

"You're the best, Pearl," she said, bending down to plant a soft kiss on the top of her kitten's head.

"Meow," Pearl said, looking up at her with big eyes. And Nia knew that meant she loved her too.

Kitten
Care Tips!

How to Groom Your Kitten

If you have a longhair kitten, you have to brush it just like Nia grooms Pearl!

Longhair cats need grooming so that their fur doesn't get knotty and matted. Shorthair cats are able to groom themselves because their hair isn't as long, but it's still important to brush them occasionally to stop them shedding too much and to keep their coats healthy – and it's a lovely way to have some extra kitten cuddles. Here's how to groom your kitten:

You will need:

- A special cat brush
- A soft blanket
- Lots of patience and love
- And your cat!

Steps:

🐾 Get a special cat brush from the vet or anywhere that sells pet supplies.

🐾 Also find a soft blanket to put on your lap. This is nice for the kitten to snuggle into, and it also protect your legs in case they start "milk treading". This is what kittens do to their mums, and it shows they're really happy, but it can still hurt if they accidentally put their claws into your lap.

🐾 Start brushing gently. Brush their back and then the sides of their body.

🐾 Remember to stroke them too and talk to them while you brush their fur.

🐾 Be very gentle when you brush their head, especially around the ears and face.

🐾 Make sure you brush behind their ears and on their tummies. This is where long-haired cats most often get matted fur.

🐾 Finish the grooming with a big cuddle and some treats!

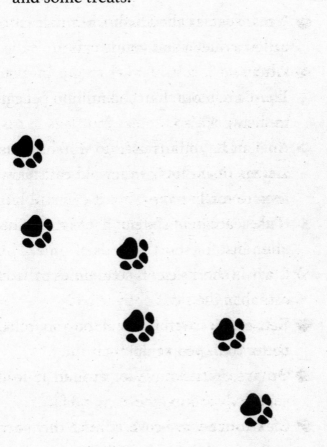

Cat Facts:

- A male cat is called a tom, a female cat is called a queen and young cats are called kittens.
- There are more than 500 million pet cats in the world.
- Ancient Egyptians used to worship cats, and there are lots of very old cat statues in museums.
- Cats sleep up to sixteen hours a day, but often just for short periods of time. This is why a short sleep is sometimes called a catnap!
- Cats can see well in the dark – six times better than people do!
- On average cats live for around 12 to 15 years.
- Cats' tongues are covered with tiny hairs that help them to clean their fur.

- Molly, Felix and Smudge are some of the most common names for a cat in the UK.
- There are over 40 different breeds of domestic cat.
- Pedigree cats like Snowflake Duchess Tippytoes can be very valuable. Persian cats are the 4th most expensive breed of cats in the world!

Big Cat, Little Cat!

As well as lions, there are lots of other types of big cat.

Lions: The best known of the big cats, lions live in groups called prides in Africa. Most wild cats are solitary, so they live on their own, but lions can live in groups because there is lots of food for them in Africa. The lionesses do the hunting, walking in a slinky, stalky way just like Nia does when she's pretending to be the cowardly lion! A lion's roar can be heard up to five miles away.

Tigers: These are the biggest cats in the world. Tigers live in India, and are very endangered. They are often killed because they eat animals that belong to farmers. Tigers are also hunted because some people wrongly believe that their bones and other parts of their bodies can be used as medicine. Tigers all have different stripes, and each animal has a different pattern. Tigers are good swimmers, and the very rare Sumatran Tiger even has webbed feet!

Cheetahs: These are the fastest animals on land. They can run up to 70 miles an hour, which is the maximum speed that cars are allowed to go on a motorway in the UK. Cheetahs don't roar like other cats – they purr instead!

Snow Leopards: Beautiful, fluffy white snow leopards are perfectly adapted to living in the freezing cold mountains. Their big furry feet act like snowshoes so they can walk over the top of the snow, rather than sinking into it.

Leopards: These live all over Asia, from China to Africa. They eat a wide range of animals, and like to take their dinner up a tree to eat it. They can carry prey that's twice as big as them.

Jaguars: These look very similar to leopards with their beautiful spots, called rosettes, but they live in America, rather than Asia.

Black Panthers: Panthers are actually just leopards or jaguars with more black pigment in their fur, so it covers their characteristic spots and gives them beautiful black fur.

There are also lots of big cats that you might not have heard of:

Servals: These are medium-sized cats that live in Africa. They mainly hunt at night to avoid bigger predators. They have beautiful spotty coats and the longest legs (compared to their body size) of all big cats.

Lynx: These have tufted bits on their ears that scientists think are like antenna to make their hearing even better. Lynx live in forests and if they have a big meal, like a deer, they then go to sleep for several days.

I sometimes feel like doing the same after a big Sunday lunch!

Ocelot: These have beautiful coats that help them hide in their jungle home, but their coats have also made them a target for poachers. Trading ocelot skins is now illegal.

Puma: A puma is also sometimes called a cougar or a mountain lion. But these cats don't live anywhere near Africa, they live in the mountains in South and North America, and Canada.

Scottish Wildcats: These are the closest of the cat family to our house cats and, as the name suggests, still live wild in Scotland. But they are very endangered, and there are very few left.

There are lots more different types of big cat around the world – and they all have similarities to our pet cats at home, with gorgeous fluffy coats, sensitive whiskers and ears, and retractable claws that make them great at climbing and catching food. When Pearl plays, she shows lots of the same behaviours as her big cat cousins. Why not see how many more big cats you can find out about?

My cats!

I have two cats called Rosie and Oscar. Even though she has a boy's name, Oscar is actually a girl cat too. My cats always come and help me when I'm writing, and sit on the keyboard with their fluffy bums. So if there are any mistakes in this book, it was probably their fault. I love them both so much. Like Nia, I always longed for a cat, and I loved it when I finally got two cats of my very own.

My dad and stepmum also have two beautiful cats called Bertie and Ritchie. Bertie has very short legs and Ritchie has a very loud miaow!

Look out for more adorable books

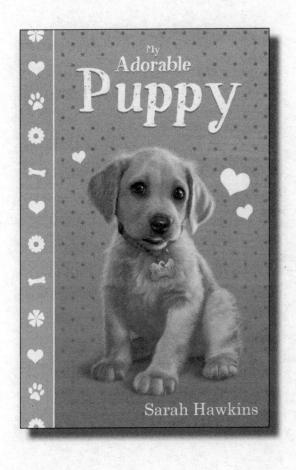

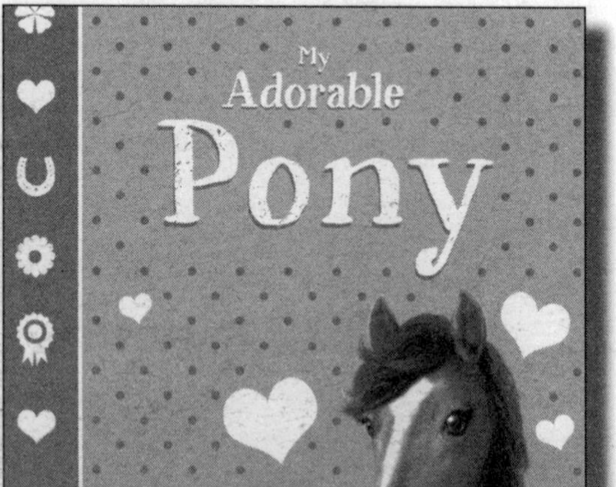
My
Adorable
Pony
Sarah Hawkins